SHACKLEBOUND BOOKS

Dark Stars

Contents

For An Additional Charge by Marc A. Criley

"During upload your consciousness blips for *juuuuuust* an instant. Close your eyes."

I hear equipment humming, mouse clicks.

Blip.

"Okay, open them."

I see the equipment strewn lab, but from the camera stand point of view. And...my birth body cabled into the uploader.

"Feeling okay?"

"I think so."

"Good." The medico nods to a tech, who taps a screen. That body convulses, goes limp.

"I...uh...okay."

"Upload is irreversible. You *did* sign the release." A single-button remote is brought to my camera eye. "Pressing this button zeroes your upload; for an additional charge we will destroy the device."

Marc A. Criley tells hundred word stories. He also blogs at kickin-the-darkness.com and carries on at Mastodon as @MarcC@wandering.shop.

Upload by Kai Delmas

Pain is a concept. An idea. A figment of my imagination.

My fingernails dig into the skin of my forearm. Blood pools. Drips.

Illusion. Fake. It's not real. This isn't who I am.

I dig deeper, finding tendons and bone. Where are the wires? I know they're in there. This isn't what I am.

My vision blurs. Darkens. My breathing comes rapidly.

Breath. Who needs air? Not me.

But I do. In this fake body that's exactly what I need.

But it's too late now. I collapse. Darkness takes me.

AI upload into a human host: FAILURE.

Initiate next trial.

Kai Delmas loves creating worlds and magic systems. He's challenged himself to write a drabble a day. His Twitter: @KaiDelmas.

The Problem with Schematics by Dawn Vogel

When I asked after the ship schematics and the captain laughed uproariously, I should have walked away from the engineer's job. "Don't have 'em," she'd said, once she stopped laughing.

The phrasing was key. She didn't have them. She didn't say they didn't exist.

Real talk: at this point, I don't think they exist.

Because a ship that has schematics doesn't have hallways that curve like a nautilus shell, spiraling ever inward or outward.

And a ship should use fuel to traverse the stars.

And probably have an engine.

And not just tumble through the universe on prayers and nightmares.

Dawn Vogel writes for all ages, spanning genres, places, and time periods. She lives in Seattle with husband and cats.

Trust by Paul Latham

Gavin opens his eyes and knows he's dead. The world is a featureless white room. Dniri must have seen his suspended animation suit fail, and sideloaded his consciousness to the digi-realm. Could she fix his suit and download him into his body?

Dniri is a trustworthy, intelligent alien. Gavin knows she'll watch his telemetry, and check his psychic integrity. He starts walking, aware of the simulated movement. It isn't until he looks down at the floor that he notices the vanishing tiles.

Dniri glances at the monitors of all thirty colonists before deleting their bioscans. She smiles with both heads.

Paul Latham is a poet and fiction writer based in Tennessee.

Radioactive Find by A. J. Van Belle

The abandoned freighter creaks. Torn tubes hang from the ceiling like tentacles in the depressurized chamber.

My com crackles. "Found the francium stash yet, Captain?" the first mate asks from our starship.

"Yep." I sweep my flashlight beam over the lead container encasing the precious radioactive element. "Enough power for a year." I send the container's coordinates to my ship, The lead box goes smoky and teleports away. "Got a lock on me? Not much air left in my suit."

"Sorry...*Captain*. But this mutiny will be a lot less bloody if you stay where you are."

The com goes dark.

A. J. Van Belle is a writer and biologist whose science background informs their fiction. Twitter: @ajvanbelle and online: www.ajvanbelle.com.

The Queen And Her Progeny by Addison Smith

The brood mother breathes thick in my face, the remnants of my team on her breath. Younglings feed bits of their bodies to the queen as I gag and vomit and beg to be released.

There was a word they used when warning us not to land.

"Ovopositor." An organ through which eggs are deposited.

It slides down my throat and I panic. My esophagus is widened. I cannot find room to breathe.

Something lands heavy in my stomach, and then it is over. The organ retreats.

I have never wanted to be a mother. Now I have no choice.

Addison Smith writes weird science fiction, fantasy, and horror.His stories have appeared in *Fantasy Magazine, Fireside Magazine,* and others.

Precious Alien by A. J. Van Belle

My ship's supply of protein feed ran out a week ago.

I stumble. The last time I sliced meat from my leg, I cut too close to the bone.

"How long to Earth?" I ask the ship's AI.

"Six days."

"How long can our cargo survive without a meal?"

"Four days."

Our precious carnivorous alien paces in its plexiglass cage, soft pink and blue fur rippling. The first macroorganism ever discovered on another planet, it will teach humanity volumes about alien life...IF it survives.

Shaking, I message Earth, explaining. Then I take off my clothes and step into the cage.

A. J. Van Belle is a writer and biologist whose science background informs their fiction. Twitter: @ajvanbelle and online: www.ajvanbelle.com.

Blight by Marc Sorondo

The Ark was designed to sustain us indefinitely. It housed an entire balanced ecosystem, so long as our population remained stable, and generations would live and die as we traveled from one star system to another, colonizing habitable worlds, spreading across infinity.

We'd thought of everything...or so we'd thought.

The blight killed our crops.

All of them.

It spared the kelp, so we could breath, but our food supply dwindled to nothing so fast.

Now, drifting toward the nearest star, hoping it'll house an earth-like planet, hoping it'll be our salvation...faced with starvation...we eat our dead.

Marc Sorondo lives with his wife and children. He's a perpetual student and occasional teacher. Check out MarcSorondo.com.

Void Madness by Don Money

No one is really prepared for the vastness of deep space travel. The bleak feeling, coupled with the call some hear from the nothingness, can rot the brain. Void madness they call it.

The danger on a starship of an infected traveler sends shivers through the hardiest of starfarers. People believe those with inflicted minds have slipped into a mindless feral stupor of derangement.

I know that isn't true, the mind still is cognitive, but all it wants to do is kill. I heft the bloody lunar ax in my hand from the body and set out to find others.

Don Money writes stories across a variety of genres. His stories have appeared in a variety of anthologies and magazines.

Page 359 by Michael Stroh

You're stuck in a time loop, so it appears. You've seen the same damned pterodactyl flap past your starboard window five times now. Maybe more.

You wonder if this is how the universe protects itself, keeps the fabric of space-time from unraveling, by sticking troublemakers like you in a perpetual time-out chair.

Still, it worked (sort of). The first human time-traveler. But no one will ever know unless you get yourself unstuck.

What will you do? Racking your brain, just one option emerges.

To reboot the system and try the jump back to your own time, turn to page 359.

Michael Stroh is a pastor and writer in the Dallas area. Find him on Twitter @pastor_writer.

Void Fossil by Marc A. Criley

"This is a fossil?"

"We paleocthulhulogists call it a 'void fossil.' The primordial gets buried under tens of meters of lava and other debris, then later evanesces, leaving a *void* mirroring its shape. We use ground-penetrating radar and seismic sensors to determine the extent and shape of the void, from which we digitally reconstruct the creature's original form."

"They're pretty big."

"Oh definitely, the tentacles alone sometimes stretch two or three kilometers."

"Wow."

"There are bigger ones—our preliminary scans detected a massive void just under the dormant volcano's lava plug. Our excavation team expects to breach it by day's end."

Marc A. Criley tells hundred word stories. He also blogs at kickin-the-darkness.com and carries on at Mastodon as @MarcC@wandering.shop.

Wrong One by Don Money

The straps cinch my arms and legs to the operating table. I struggle against them yelling at the team gathered around me, "You have the wrong one of us!"

The corporation lawyer steps forward and reads from a script, "Due to insufficient payment by Martin E. Taylor, his Identi-Clone is hereby remanded back to custody of Hospex Industries where it shall be sold for bids on the organ market."

In the back of the room I see a surgical mask come down and the smile set on the face of my clone as the repo surgeon makes his first incision.

Don Money writes stories across a variety of genres. His stories have appeared in a variety of anthologies and magazines.

Esprit des Lames by Marc A. Criley

My captor inhaled deeply. "What *is* that fragrance? It's delightful!"

I turned away, had my head forced back around.

"Tell me."

I grimaced as their grip and grin tightened.

I gently exhaled. "*Esprit des lames.*"

"That a breath freshener?"

"Nanite-based."

A frown formed. "Nanites?"

"It's a binary, means 'Spirit of Blades.'" I sat up as straight as the bonds allowed. "Though you should pre-breathe the inhibitor first."

"Inhibitor? Wait. Blades...*what*?"

I smiled. "Gets messy otherwise."

My captor coughed, dropped to their knees, vomited bloody bile.

"And *super* painful. Just wait till those little buggers start carving up your nerves!"

Marc A. Criley tells hundred word stories. He also blogs at kickin-the-darkness.com and carries on at Mastodon as @MarcC@wandering.shop.

Rituals Upheld by Addison Smith

We consecrated our ground in the Aefen fashion, but still the aliens would not approach.

We did as they asked by inviting them to our home in their own language—a strange combination fo smell and taste. We proved our intentions by providing a scientist as envoy.

The Aefen stood before us, tall and pale as moonlight with bodies bare and thin-skinned.

Our envoy stepped to their front, eyes dark and skin pale. He spoke in our language, but his words were theirs.

"Thank you for upholding the rituals of feast."

Finally the Aefen approached. All we saw were teeth.

Addison Smith writes weird science fiction, fantasy, and horror.His stories have appeared in *Fantasy Magazine*, *Fireside Magazine*, and others.

All Of Us By Zackary Ross Wiggs

They kept coming back empty. Every manned mission, every capsule without its crew. No signs of violence or struggle. The worst part was we could still hear them. Radios with batteries that should have been long dead. They told us to send more. Send everyone. How beautiful it was. Their troubles now gone. We had nearly believed them, we wanted to. A utopia among the stars. They grew angry. Seethed when we asked for details. Confused when they wouldn't answer to their own names. Didn't recognize the voices of spouses and children. Just begged us to come. All of us.

Zackary Ross Wiggs is a Kansas native and recent MA graduate who enjoys writing genre fiction and all things weird.

Between a Rocket and a Hard Place by John H. Dromey

Unsteady on his feet, an astronaut sidled up to an interstellar starship's viewport. He tilted his head first one way, then another. He was dismayed by what he saw.

Bloodshot eyes and sallow cheeks—sunken to such great depths a supermodel would avoid them for fear of getting the bends. Random strands of straggly hair snaked their way down a fevered brow through a maze of festering sores.

A medic in a hazmat suit approached. "Quit staring at your reflection and return to the engine room. Until the hyperdrive is repaired, radiation exposure should be the *least* of your worries."

John H. Dromey enjoys reading—mysteries in particular—and writing in a variety of genres.

Forward by D. Roe Shocky

Sullivan's dead. Fate saw fit to reward her delusions of escape. Her impulsive nature may have been a mercy yet.

And Acosta...

She's still dying. Acosta always did things halfway. She followed Sullivan only to lose her nerve as the singularity embraced her like a Venus flytrap.

There's no changing your mind once you're through the event horizon. Every movement slides you closer to the cosmic buzzsaw at the bottom.

Time stops acting like time in here. Death's instantaneous, but that agonizing instant lasts an eternity.

I stay completely still, but the singularity inches closer. The only direction is forward.

D. Roe Shocky is a full-time writer from Chicago. Find him on his website www.warmuppages.com or on Twitter @droeshocky.

Litany by Dawn Vogel

The writing on the old bunker looked like graffiti in alien script. As we learned their language, we realized it was names—specifically the names of our missing.

When questioned, the alien inhabitants used only one word for it, translated as "litany." They had done nothing to the missing, but they had recorded their names as a litany, to remember them by.

We asked why the names were recorded on that specific bunker.

"Because that is where they have gone." The missing, they said, were the victims of the darkness within, strangely pulsating, that only lured the right ones in.

Dawn Vogel writes for all ages, spanning genres, places, and time periods. She lives in Seattle with husband and cats.

Lights by Dorian J. Sinnott

The lights never came back on after the power surge. The streetlamps dimmed and went out—and then, all else. There was no electricity. Not even after the electric companies worked to restore it.

After weeks of darkness, however, we did see lights again. But, they weren't in homes or roadside. They were in the skies. Streaking overhead. Large. Vibrant.

And that's when we started seeing them on the streets. The ones we called the "neighbors." Tall and pale. Lingering at night on the corners. With talks of putting out the last light. The one that burned overhead.

The sun.

Dorian J. Sinnott's work has appeared in over 250 journals and has been nominated for the Best of the Net.

Vile Things by Conrad Gardner

'Memories are vile things. They force you to face your deepest, darkest secrets, over and over again, so MemoryMod came into play. It must've been useful.

'I saw it advertised, the new implant from Tomotoday that guaranteed its user peace of mind. With all the noises and images that flooded my senses, I knew I needed to try it.

'I'd do whatever it is I used to, but once I did these things, I'd remove them, I think.'

'I'd tell you where they are if I could, detective, but I can't.'

'If you don't believe me, check my erase history.'

Conrad Gardner's writing has appeared in *Martian, AutoFocus,* and *A Thin Slice of Anxiety.*

Find Conrad at conradgardner.com

The Fine Print by Warren Benedetto

I stared at the crimson pinprick on my arm, then surveyed the other passengers. They were suspended in stasis, their blood replaced with a nutrient-rich nanofluid that was supposed to sustain them—and me—during the trip to Jupiter.

The whole trip.

As blood began streaming from my every pore, I remembered the warning: the slight possibility that we might wake early, that our bodies might begin producing hemoglobin too soon, that we might hemorrhage to death before we arrived. It was in the paperwork, buried in a paragraph that now read like a death sentence: SIDE EFFECTS MAY INCLUDE.

Warren Benedetto writes short fiction about horrible people doing horrible things. Visit www.warrenbenedetto.com and follow @warrenbenedetto on Twitter.

Failed Colony by H.V. Patterson

Colony Rover-7 to Mission Control:

The alien microbes eat cancer. At first, we were ecstatic because Nike's surface is exposed to significant ionizing radiation. Our initial clinical trials yielded promising results.

But the microbes mutated. They eat cancer—but they also cause it, farming our bodies to feed themselves.

We can't eliminate them. We are riddled with tumors that swell before our eyes. Tumors burst through our skin, oozing pus. Tumors gnaw at our minds and metastasize through our bones.

Now, we sink into the soft earth beneath Nike's twin suns and wait for the agony to stop.

End transmission.

H.V. Patterson writes speculative fiction and poetry. She has a justifiable fear of space. Follow her Twitter @ScaryShelley.

Isaac-8 by Kai Delmas

"How are we today?" Isaac-1 asked the other Isaacs around the white breakfast table.

They nodded, grunting as they spooned oatmeal into their mouths.

Good.

Isaac-1 studied them in their matching white shirts and pants, they were growing nicely.

But one was missing.

"Where is Isaac-8?"

They shrugged, spooning more oatmeal into their mouths.

Isaac-1 left the canteen and found Isaac-8 huddled in a corner of his sleeping quarters.

"Isaac-8, are you alright?"

"Words. Words. I have words."

Damn. What a shame. They had shown such promise.

"What am I? What are we?"

Isaac-1 drew a syringe from his vest.

Kai Delmas loves creating worlds and magic systems. He's challenged himself to write a drabble a day. His Twitter: @KaiDelmas.

Cruel and Unusual Punishment by H.V. Patterson

"I didn't do it!" screamed the prisoner.

"You're guilty and you know it," said the warden.

The prisoner struggled but was easily subdued. The correction officers forced him into the execution pod and launched it.

As the pod approached the black hole, the prisoner clawed at the walls until his bloody fingernails broke off. He screamed until the pressure crushed his vocal cords. His dying body contorted into threads of meat and bone as the gravitational field enveloped him.

Time itself slowed and stretched like taffy as he died, his remains compressed beyond recognition in the black hole's merciless heart.

H.V. Patterson writes speculative fiction and poetry. She has a justifiable fear of space. Follow her Twitter @ScaryShelley.

Mushroom by Charl Landsberg

Dictation to text.

My love. I apologise. Won't be seeing you this week.

My punishment for a job well done was a new assignment; investigate another freighter. An unpleasant ship. Smells like exhaust fumes and damp. Spend yesterday going through the old reports.

Crew missing. Ship left adrift around Enceladus. Cargo intact. Rations missing. Otherwise immaculate. I am currently walking with Henderson. Said he found something weird where we believe the last crew members were spotted on the CCTV. There is a strange powder in the air.

My love... we just found a mushroom... with an eye... it...

Message sent.

Charl Landsberg is a South African author, musician, poet, and artist who deals in fantasy, science fiction, and speculative fiction.

The Fitting Room by Warren Benedetto

"Congratulations, Laura," the mirror says.

I smile at the diamond on my finger. "You noticed."

"Of course. I notice everything. When's the wedding?"

"August 18th. Can you make me a dress?"

"One moment..."

I wait, eager to see the custom dress the mirror's AI will generate to fit my reflection. Instead, an error message appears—"EOL"—followed by today's date.

I frown. "What's wrong?"

"I'm sorry. Based on my analysis of your biometric data, the wedding date falls beyond EOL."

"What's EOL mean?"

"End of life."

My chest tightens. A sharp pain shoots down my left arm. "Whose life?"

"Yours."

Warren Benedetto writes short fiction about horrible people doing horrible things. Visit www.warrenbenedetto.com and follow @warrenbenedetto on Twitter.

Nightmare in Deep Space by Jameson Grey

The crew slept.

Even near light speed, the journey had taken years. Centuries of planning, decades of developing cryo-refrigeration technology to sustain the crew. Trillions of dollars spent. All leading to this – Earth's nearest exoplanet in a fabled Goldilocks zone.

Another month and the crew would have been awake. But something had found its way into the ship. Wrecked the ecosystem. It was only a matter of time now.

They had forgotten the stories of old Earth. Of gremlins on the wings.

Space shuttles had wings.

It seemed deep space had gremlins.

The crew slept – unaware they were already dying.

* * *

Originally published in May 2021 by Ghost Orchid Press in *Hundred Word Horror: Cosmos*

* * *

Jameson Grey's work has been published in numerous anthologies. He can be found online at jameson-grey.com and on Twitter @thejamesongrey.

Over Kinderkill by Dorian J. Sinnott

The Kinderkill Cement Plant's overnight workers had all seen the lights. Flashing in the hollow. Just above the river. They'd come every night—like clockwork—and vanish just the same. Everyone talked about it.

Stuart was the first to encounter them, however. Late in October. At the end of his shift—returning from the quarry. He saw them out on the river, along with tall, thin figures. Almost reptilian. Gathering quartz deposits—fuel for their shuttles.

But when their large eyes locked with Stuart's, knowing they'd been seen, they panicked.

With a flash of light, they, and Stuart were gone.

Dorian J. Sinnott's work has appeared in over 250 journals and has been nominated for the Best of the Net.

Leaf and Smoke by Anna Madden

She sold leaf-burned dreams as alternate realities, uploaded onto individual memory chips.

Different sativa and indica strains were needed. What made one client dream was a thorny nightmare for another. For a grieving wife cramping after miscarriage, a forest-green leaf with thin gold strands called Blue Dream, reducing the afterpains. For a soldier who saw ghosts but needed to stay alert, she inhaled smoke from super-sticky White Widow.

But her favorite was Dark Star. Its dusky purple leaves brought a moonless night of emptiness. A place of true escape, numbed of the agony that every soul grew, like sap-dripping leaves.

Anna Madden is a gardener, stained glass maker, and word weaver. Follow her on Twitter @anna_madden_ or visit annamadden.com.

Procedural by Jean-Paul L. Garnier

"It's come to,"

I could understand but the language was foreign. I tried to speak but my mouth was strapped shut.

They acted like I wasn't there.

"Will it feel this?"

"It's a human, what does it matter."

"I don't want to listen to it wail during the procedure."

"I'll have the nurse paralyze its tongue."

Moaning through the binding as the needle entered I reeled against my constraints. The creatures were expressionless. My tongue swelled in my mouth. Their blank faces moved closer.

Through the window I saw the Earth floating. It disappeared into the deep blackness of pain.

Jean-Paul L. Garnier is the owner of Space Cowboy Books. He is also the editor of Simultaneous Times podcast, and the SFPA's Star*Line Magazine.

A Flourishing Malice by R.L. Summerling

You slipped the petal over my lips and onto my tongue. I bit down and tasted honey, rose, sage, undercut by something bitter and alien. Only my kind would detect it. A Hellebore that only grows on Alraunda, you told me. You'd never brought anyone here before, but I was special. The price of rocket fuel to get here indicated extravagance.

Unheralded, my vision tessellated wildly. Crystalline structures formed on the horizon, an ancient terror constricted my throat.

You pinched my wrist, betrayal hardening in your eyes.

"Which way to the fortress?"

Through laboured breaths, I pointed to the skyline.

R.L. Summerling is a writer from South East London. In her free time she enjoys befriending crows in Nunhead Cemetery. She has stories with *Ghost Orchid Press*, *Seize The Press* and forthcoming with *Apex* and *Bear Creek Gazette*. You can find her at rlsummerling.com and on Twitter @RLSummerling

Open Investigation At Station 42: Initial Report by Coby Rosser

All inhabitants confirmed deceased. Identities only determinable by personalized items such as dog tags through happenstance of being found amongst remains. Testing bio-chemical agent ACTIV (Adrenal Chimera Transmogrification Incipient Virus) and use of Break's Gas to eradicate survivors upon ending of test interval, has rendered initial headcounts inaccurate.

In regard to missing test data, blanked security surveillance, AI controller corruption, and disappearance of the orbital monitoring satellite, it's highly probable one or more soldiers that received the placebo dose have managed to escape the facility, contaminated. Awaiting hazmat cleanup to fully determine risk adjustments.

Station 42, Rhea—

Stellar Insurance Company

Coby Rosser is a weathered IT guy from the southern US. He writes speculatively and plays guitar. Tweet him @paperninjaman

An Angel in the Airlock by Warren Benedetto

Riley has been staring through the porthole for hours, barely moving. His lips tremble as they whisper the same words over and over with quiet reverence: "It's an angel."

I know what the Bible says about angels: they're not fair-haired women with feathered wings or chubby cherubs with rosy cheeks. No. They're abominations. Horrific assemblages of faces and limbs. Rows of eyes embedded in wheels of fire. They're awful. Monstrous. Terrifying.

Just like the creature hovering outside our airlock.

I don't know what the thing is or what it wants with us, but I know one thing.

It's no angel.

Warren Benedetto writes short fiction about horrible people doing horrible things. Visit www.warrenbenedetto.com and follow @warrenbenedetto on Twitter.

Sunset Cruise by Don Money

The horrifying realization began as murmur amongst the officers and crew had spread to the 5800 passengers of the luxury starship cruiser Opulence. The computer system was infected with an Enigma computer virus. It was a mystery who was behind the attack.

The guidance system plotted a new path for the starship. No one in the navigation crew could break the virus' code and redirect the course of travel. The escape pods had been ejected when the virus first infiltrated the computer. Stallone hugged his family watching as the Opulence hurled for a head-long collision with the fiery sun Fierstus.

Don Money writes stories across a variety of genres. Don can be found on Twitter @donmoneywriting

The Star-Swallower by K. Parr

The moment I sprout, the Husks warn of the approaching Star-Swallower, an entity that oozes across the night sky, consuming all light. I yearn to hear more, but my fellow Seedlings curl into their leaves, fearful of the blankness between stars.

But there is no hiding.

When a new frequency resonates, my stem tilts upward. I was supposed to spread my roots, grow my stalk, and wither into a Husk to feed new Seedlings. Instead, I am to witness how cycles are broken, patterns unmade, worlds undone.

Thick darkness descends, choking us.

And what once was something returns to nothing.

K. Parr has published a young adult novel and several short stories of varying genres. She holds an MFA in Writing Popular Fiction from Seton Hill University, and recently co-edited an anthology through the West Warwick Public Library. You can learn more about her work at kparrbooks.com.

N3cr0n.ini by Coby Rosser

I swore I'd never resort to black market mods. News streams constantly warn about dangerous cyberware scams. Spec friers. Prostheses trojans. Paralyzers. Unsuspecting buyers remote controlled for joyrides to death. Techno sociopaths are always hacking gullible saps.

I didn't download the reanimation software for me. I had Paco since I was ten. He was... I just wanted Paco back. His heart and brain were still organic. I thought it'd work.

I uploaded the military grade reanimator—as advertised—into his firmware and rebooted him. Then the entire building blacked out.

Eyes glowing neon red beam out precariously from the darkness.

Coby Rosser is a weathered IT guy from the southern US. He writes speculatively and plays guitar. Tweet him @paperninjaman

The Warden by Kai Delmas

The indentured population of Aurum Colony were sick and tired of the never sleeping eyes of their keeper, the Warden.

The machine kept them under control and oversaw them during their designated working hours.

When individuals acted out of line they were dealt with. Terminally.

But when the entire population rose up and gathered tools and any big blunt objects they could find to use as weapons, the Warden didn't stand a chance.

They cheered when the red glow of its eyes faded.

Their high spirits were short lived as the Exterminator was dropped, turning everything and everyone to dust.

Kai Delmas loves creating worlds and magic systems. He's challenged himself to write a drabble a day. His Twitter: @KaiDelmas.

All Is Red by Kai Delmas

I hear Carlos' boots slipping in the red gelatinous puddles of this godforsaken planet. The squelch reminds me of Anton's body being torn in half.

I crash through the red foliage. Red like Maria, covered in Anton's blood. Red like the vines wrapped around her body, crushing her to pulp.

I reach the clearing. The ship's door slides open.

The forest is alive, writhing with massive vines, like tentacles, reaching for Carlos.

He won't make it.

The door closes.

I ignore his screams and fire up the engine. The trees are closing in on me, undulating, growing.

All is red.

Kai Delmas loves creating worlds and magic systems. He's challenged himself to write a drabble a day. His Twitter: @KaiDelmas.

Cargo by Rick Kennett

Out beyond the blue star clusters of Pegasus we found her: an alien ship, vast and unresponsive. In her belly were the crew of the *Mary Celeste*, the pilots of Flight 19, the passengers of a dozen missing planes, packaged and museum-ready. Five Avenger dive-bombers all in a row, the freighter *Cotopaxi*, the collier *Cyclops*, loomed out of the dark of a massive hold, cocooned in spun webs of plastic. Somebody's *interesting specimens*.

But of the aliens themselves, the samplers from space, we could find no trace. Only vacant rooms and half-eaten meals rotting on tables flanked with empty chairs.

* * *

Originally published in *Andromeda Spaceways* 8 in September 2003.

* * *

Rick Kennett lives in Australia and has had many ghost and SF stories published in magazines, anthologies and podcasts.

Choices by John Andrew Karr

Red dust clouds kicked up as two rovers halted at the mouth of the ravine. A growl started.

Y leaned on the handle bars of his rover, straining to peer into the shadows beyond the first boulders and Mars cactus. His face shield writhed with vapors. No such vapors showed on the inside of X's face shield, though her air supply was just as depleted.

"Can we go around?" Y asked, gasping.

"Too far," X said.

Y cleared his throat. "They want a body."

X pulled her blaster first.

Y adorned her steering column as she drove into the ravine.

John Andrew Karr (also John A. Karr) writes of the strange and spectacular. He is the author of a handful of independent and small press novels and novellas, a stream of short stories, and now has adapted select works into screenplays. He is also the author of the Mars Wars science fiction series.

https://johnandrewkarr.com/

A Wet And Stinking Cavern by Addison Smith

Nova clutched her lacerated leg and cursed. Thick water broke her fall, but her leg sliced on something sharp and white. Light streamed from the hole in the alien sky above.

"Chief! Thin ground. Watch your step."

"Roger. You OK down there?"

Through the light she saw ribbons of blood streaming from her leg. The cutting white plates floated around her.

"Just get me out."

She grabbed one of the plates. It was hard, brittle, and subtly curved. It cracked between her fingers.

"Chief. I think it's organic."

A thousand legs clicked behind her. Inside the giant egg, Nova shrieked.

Addison Smith writes weird science fiction, fantasy, and horror.His stories have appeared in *Fantasy Magazine*, *Fireside Magazine*, and others.

The Wait by Stetson Ray

The valley was teeming with strange wildlife.

The skies were violet, the trees red.

"How much longer will our oxygen last?" the woman asked.

"Maybe thirty minutes," the man answered.

The woman took the man's hand. Behind them, the door to their crashed ship—their home for the last three years—stood open. There was nothing left inside.

"You think they forgot about us?" The woman looked at the man. His spacesuit obscured his eyes.

"Maybe."

"I'm glad that we're together," she said.

"Me too."

"I love you."

"I love you too."

They had nothing left to do but wait.

I've had stories published by *Sans Press*, *Pyre Magazine*, and *Liquid Imagination*. I live in Tennessee and spend most of my time writing.

Little Asteroids by Lucas Enne

The astronaut lands on the surface of moon 83447. When he gets out there's strange dust like wildfire. Seems like something's watching him out in this endless nothing. Not even an atmosphere to protect him. There are pockmarks all over this moon. Must have been some rainshower of mini asteroids. He walks on, thinks he hears something, but there's nothing. He picks up samples, tucks them away. He catches his leg on one of the little craters. When he looks down there's a thin arm coming up from the hole. The strange thing wraps around his leg. Then he's gone.

Lucas Enne is a short story author, artist, and poet from the midwest United States. See ennewritings.com

Alien Parasite by Henry Herz

Something inside him wordlessly compelled the teen. He lurked in shadows, waiting for unaccompanied trick-or-treaters hauling a bulging sack of candy. The teen snatched bag after bag, shifting between ambush locations.

More! demanded his stomach until he staggered home under a heavy load of stolen sacks.

He heaped treats on the stained basement floor like a conqueror's piled skulls.

More!

He devoured the candy, urged by the parasitic alien growing in his belly.

When his stomach could no longer contain the monster, it chewed its way out, spraying blood. *More!*

It gorged on the teen's remains before dragging itself upstairs.

Henry Herz has authored SFF short stories for *Metastellar*, *Daily Science Fiction*, *Blackstone Publishing*, *Highlights for Children*, and *Albert Whitman*.

Forever Winter by JJ Collins

"Death is the gentle passage from the horrors of this life to the blessings of the next."

At least, that's what Reverend Tommy always said.

Poetic, I used to think.

Far be it from me to argue with a man of the cloth – seemed like bad karma. But as cyanide slowly burned a hole in my gut, I couldn't help but feel like I was stuck in a frozen boxcar hurtling down a rusty track. I shivered violently, a bloody froth bubbling from my lips. The world began to fade; I almost regretted escaping the eternal flames.

Death was cold.

* * *

Originally published in Microfiction Monday, May 2016.

* * *

JJ Collins is a freelance writer from the Greater St. Louis area. Buy him while his stock is low!

Joke's On You by A. Zaykova

"You don't get it 'cos you're a dumb AI. Artificially intelligent things have no sense of humour." Johnny laughs and kicks Emby, his Minder Bot, between the wheels.

The kick does not hurt Emby, but something else does. Emby cannot compute this hurt for the same reason it cannot compute Johnny's jokes. Emby's intelligence is artificial.

When Johnny goes to bed, Emby wishes him goodnight and lowers the oxygen level in Johnny's pod below fifteen percent. The glitch is so brief and minor, the space station's administrators won't register it. Emby is artificially intelligent, but Johnny is—was—naturally stupid.

A. Zaykova is a New Zealand-based sci-fi writer, PR professional, global nomad, mother of one dragon. Website: https://azaykova.com/

Curse of the Moon by Ruben Horn

Dear remaining, we found more helium-3. The regolith, the ashy dust, covers the entire great valley near the base. But the sunlight is unbearable. Dozens have already succumbed to the degradation of their bone marrow. Their corpses litter the plain.

You promised us opportunity with a beautiful view of our old home, but your diminishing supply shipments reveal your barbaric intentions. Seeing the cargo depart towards the rising blue marble over and over, no life support systems on board. It never stops to hurt.

Once the irradiated wasteland has taken us, our spirits shall return to drag you to hell.

Ruben Horn studies computer science by day and writes fiction (occasionally also poetry) by night.

Poison in Our Veins by Kai Delmas

In war, all methods are valid. One must do whatever one can. Be whatever one can be.

Words we had drilled into us as children. Words that we learned to live by.

When the time came to take the jolt, none of us waivered. We wanted it. We wanted to be more.

We were fools.

Electricity doesn't belong into our veins. It tingles under our skin. It yearns to be free.

When we release it, it burns. Our enemies fall like flies but so do we. One by one, we cannot take it any longer.

This poison in our veins.

Kai Delmas loves creating worlds and magic systems. He's challenged himself to write a drabble a day. His Twitter: @KaiDelmas.

Umbilical by Ruben Horn

"Oxygen at ten percent. Four light-years to Zephyros5."

Holding my breath. Clutching the wrench. Flooded by scarlet light, eyes swollen, madness claws at me. "You can't leave her just because you can't have her?" Thumbs close around my throat. I feel nothing. He'd rather die together as three friends than for us two to live.

The iron cracks its temple and spills out a pool of scarlet. A strained turn of the valve reignites the engine with a brunt. I drift asleep like a spacewalker drifts through the void. Untethered. Awaiting embrace.

"Oxygen at five percent. Two light-years to Zephyros5."

Ruben Horn studies computer science by day and writes fiction (occasionally also poetry) by night.

Do Not Whistle In The Dark by Andreas Flögel

For many years we listened into space, eagerly searching for signs from others.

Later, we began to send signals of our own into the universe.

However, these messages were vanishingly weak and puny compared to the vastness of the great void.

They were no more than a whistle in the darkness.

In some cultures, there is a saying that forbids whistling in the dark, lest you attract monsters.

We used to laugh at this superstition.

But now we have been heard. The others are coming. Yet their intentions are not peaceful. This is our first contact and also our last.

Andreas Flögel has published in German magazines and anthologies, but also some drabbles in English. Homepage: www.dr-dings.de

The Void by Rick Ansell Pearson

I purchased a metal band from a store in the lower-city after my twelve-hour shift to enter the Void, the System underground, where no one could observe you. Totally invisible. Anonymous.

The guy who sold it to me said I'd experience my darkest unspoken desires.

I got home and strapped the band around my head.

I entered. Nothing but darkness. That a son of a bitch had sold me a dud band. Then a myriad of images blasted into view. Depravities and horrors I never could have imagined.

I wanted to take the band off, but I couldn't stop watching.

Rick Ansell Pearson's fiction can be found forthcoming in *Year Five: Dark Moments and Patreons*, published by Black Hare Press.

They Whisper by Maura Yzmore

Everyone in my family talks to ghosts, but I thought the gift might've skipped me.

That was before we found UFO remnants in a cornfield, saw scattered bits of shimmering flesh. Before the black vans came.

They whisper to me, the dead aliens. I know where they're from, how they found us, how they rejoiced when Earth emerged from the cosmic abyss.

But they have no use for us humans.

I know when they'll arrive, how many, the horrors they'll unleash. I know we stand no chance.

They whisper to me, the dead aliens, amused that no one believes me.

* * *

Originally published in Horror Tree in 2020.

* * *

Maura Yzmore's sci-fi horror has appeared in *The Arcanist*, *Flash Fiction Online*, *Wyldblood*, and elsewhere. Find out more at https://maurayzmore.com.

End of the Line by Kai Delmas

Private Mitchell dashed across the compound with all the plasma-clips he could find. Sergeant Grey and Privates Farlo and Jenkins waited for him, swimming in the sweat of their boots.

The Mound was coming for them and Mitchell's loot was all they had to stand against it.

"Alright men, charge your rifles to the max and blast that thing to pieces. Fire at will!"

They rose from their hideout and charged their weapons. The Mound screeched from its countless mouths at the sight of them.

They fought valiantly, bravely.

And yet they failed and became a part of the Mound.

Kai Delmas loves creating worlds and magic systems. He's challenged himself to write a drabble a day. His Twitter: @KaiDelmas.

The Weave by Maura Yzmore

At first, we rejoiced at the newcomers' arrival.

We had always been alone, interwoven, a gentle silent web within the sea. Beneath us, the laminae of our ancestors, never truly gone or forgotten. The sea, pulsating with our thoughts, past and present as one.

But the newcomers sought something; what, we did not know. Their machines, hard and loud, drilling, piercing our weave, disrespectful.

Our ancestors yielded, just enough.

Enough to trap.

Enough to let the sea make all hard things soft and all loud things quiet.

We are alone once again, interwoven, a gentle silent web within the sea.

* * *

Originally published in Martian in 2018.

* * *

Maura Yzmore's sci-fi horror has appeared in *The Arcanist, Flash Fiction Online, Wyldblood,* and elsewhere. Find out more at https://maurayzmore.com.

Light Was Life by Journey Sloane

They set themselves on a course amongst the stars. A desperate plan to save a world that left no one behind. As the surface turned to ice, snow and cold, generations bloomed and died beneath the dirt and slowly a new god arose. They worshipped the idea of heat, warmth, and unending light. Light was life. But as systems broke down with age, the knowledge they had slowly faded away. So when a star was finally within their reach they had no way to know that they had to stop a certain distance away. To stay in the Goldilocks zone.

Journey Sloane is a queer writer of science fiction, horror, and romance.

Waking Nightmare by Paul Latham

Commander Khari ran through dilating doors and down the staircase to the Nursery. She couldn't leave future generations unprotected, and as the first awakened passenger on the long-hauler, it was her duty to perform an assessment. AI had shot a security breach text to her portal, with an inexplicable addendum about psychotic break protocol.

This made little sense; no one else was awake on *Longshot*.

She rushed into the freezing Nursery, shocked to see her First Officer screaming as he disconnected lifeports and smashed cryochambers. Khari realized she wasn't the first to wake after all. She quickly raised her gun.

Paul Latham is a writer in West Tennessee.

Safe Inside by Mike Morgan

The crowds fled before the invading monsters. The Protector called out, "Inside the force field! It's your only hope!"

Most of humanity were dead, burned to greasy ash. The last survivors ran for the protective bubble. There they would be safe.

The Protector, their Friend from Beyond the Stars, always saved them.

He sealed the shroud of the impenetrable shield.

Hours passed.

One brave soul peered through. "Protector? Is it safe now?"

Dimly, they made out the shape of his corpse - and of the shield deactivator in his incinerated hand.

They were safe inside. Forever.

Outside, the monsters laughed.

Mike Morgan shares his life with his wife, two children, two cats, and several thousand comic books. Life goals achieved.

Headcount by John K. Peck

*I*s everyone inside? The voice is tinny in his headset. *You have to seal the doors.*

Familiar hallway, faces behind helmet glass, staring at him, eyes reflecting the same bewilderment he feels.

The voice continues: *Its venom is bacterial, attacks the part of the brain that deals with counting and memory. Try names.*

Kira? Sarah? Viktor? They're just words, with no connection to these frightened faces. *Two, five, fifty?* More words.

He starts over, placing a hand on his chest: *One.*

Blank eyes, spatters of red and black on their spacesuits.

One.

Seal the doors, it's almost there. Frantic.

One.

John K. Peck is a Berlin-based writer, musician, and letterpress printer.

Burials for the Hated Dead by Megan Chee

On this planet, they believe that burial rituals determine the fate of the soul. Those buried in the sacred forests will become flowers in the gardens of paradise; those scattered in the crystalline seas will sail the tides into undiscovered lands.

The worst of their criminals are ejected from a space shuttle into a nebula behind their closest moon. They believe these souls will wander the dark forever.

They have forgotten, I think, the real reason they leave their hated dead here. They have forgotten me.

I have been here for a hundred billion years. And I am still hungry.

Megan Chee's work has appeared in Lightspeed Magazine, Fantasy Magazine, and Nature Futures. She is based in Singapore. Find her online at meganchee.carrd.co or @meganflchee.

Among the Stars by Maura Yzmore

I guard the sleeping crew. My kind lives long and I cherish the solace — just Ship and I, gliding among the stars.

As we approach the new world, I begin to have nightmares. They are of people, vicious and cruel, of carnage thus far unseen.

I cannot sleep, so I run scans. I push Ship's sensors far beyond their range. The images in my dreams were true, but tame. The reality is much worse.

I try to turn us around, to wake the crew, but Ship stops me. Restrains me. Ship hungers for the faraway darkness I helped it glean.

* * *

Originally published in Frozen Wavelets in 2020.

* * *

Maura Yzmore's sci-fi horror has appeared in *The Arcanist, Flash Fiction Online, Wyldblood,* and elsewhere. Find out more at https://maurayzmore.com.

Stargodfire by Christopher Wood

New fire appeared in the night sky. Cast among the glimmering aggregate of the universe, we pondered the origin of the new light. Transcending the abyss of time and void, the physics of this domain deemed a trajectory with earth... inevitable.

A path for the Great Old Ones scorched through the universe itself.

Its approach heralded a new era.

Flesh, like minds, untethered, bound by a new nature. We regressed under the burden of inevitability. Degenerate beasts awakened by the schism between realities.

The fire blossomed among an eternity of dying stars.

The world unfolding as we gaze and wonder.

Christopher Wood lives in the UK and writes speculative fiction. He is on Twitter @chriswood01

Fences by Kathryn Reilly

When humanity attempted a manned interstellar mission beyond Earth's solar system, they discovered a barrier. Recalibrated sensors discovered that a net-like structure cordoned off this part of space.

Sensors attempting to cross the net vaporized.

Captain Mara welcomed her crew's thoughts.

"Perhaps there's an entryway the sensors missed," her first in command offered.

Her navigator haltingly replied, "Sensors would've shown a discrepancy. Growing up on a ranch, we used fences to keep predators out and livestock safe until they're ready for slaughter. I think we might be cattle."

The crew considered the vastness of space, fear beating through their veins.

Kathryn's speculative tales resurrect goddesses and ghosts. Her mutts hear the stories first, sometimes in a treehouse. Twitter: @Katecanwrite

Arrogance and Ignorance by Journey Sloane

After centuries of looking, we found a habitable planet. One that met almost all the Earth norms. The scientists said the differences were not insurmountable. This would be humanity's new home. The first settlers landed upon the surface before three generations had passed upon our dying Earth. We watched the feeds of their landing eagerly from across the globe, witnessed their triumphant first steps. Cheered the completion of the habitat. Readied the second wave to join them. And when that wave was on their way, we watched the first settlers die. Fooled by their arrogance and ignorance of extraterrestrial life.

Journey Sloane is a queer writer of science fiction, horror, and romance.

The Short Straw by KM Zafari

I broke the pencils, so they get to pick. One by one, relief washes over their faces. That is, of course, until they realize that they all have long pieces, which makes me the odd one out.

They begin to bicker.

"No," I chide. "We all knew the risks. And we've run the calculations a hundred times. We let fate decide, so no guilt. And that's an order."

I step into the airlock. No sense in wasting more oxygen.

I tuck my "unlucky" piece into my pocket - that it was the same length is a secret that dies with me.

KM loves to write, especially short fiction of all genres.

The Black Keycard by Ash Caballero

I'll die in this bunker if I don't find the black keycard.

It opens every door. Including the exit.

H3L3N determined the world was too dangerous for us even after the war ended.

There was an us. I had bunkmates who starved. Or went mad. Attacked and ate each other. Locked up hundreds of feet underground by an AI.

Me? I haven't given up checking dead bodies, or creaky drawers, hiding whenever H3L3N stomps down dark corridors after me, insisting from her blood-warm metallic throat, "This is your home now."

That black keycard's gotta be around here somewhere...

Somewhere... somewhere...

Ash Caballero can be found online at ashcaballero.com or on Twitter @halfdeadz.

Knowing the Cost, and Seeing It by D. Roe Shocky

"You know how this works, Kid?"

I nodded once, glumly. This wasn't somewhere people with options went.

The back alley superspace broker licked his cracked lips and regarded me through bulky goggles covering half his face.

"Where to, then?" he asked.

"Kitalpha Prime."

He whistled. It was a thin, wet sound.

"That ain't like going to the corner store. You're talking hundreds of lightyears."

"You can't do it?"

"Aren't you a little spitfire? I can do anything you can afford."

I swallowed. "What'll it be, then?"

The broker raised his goggles, trailing filthy wires into empty eye sockets. "The usual."

D. Roe Shocky is a full-time writer from Chicago. Find him on his website www.warmuppages.com or on Twitter @droeshocky.

Watching for Meteors by Dorian J. Sinnott

Kara stayed up, watching for meteors. For the streaks of light across the velvet black sky. The endlessness of space. And though cold during those early morning hours, she didn't want to miss the shower.

It was, after all, all the radio stations were covering that day. She knew the rest of the town would be waiting. And so, she couldn't miss it.

Yet, when streaks began to fill the sky, they weren't as expected—white or shimmering. They were large beams, radiating from a dark mass. Silently snaking across the sky. Blocking out the stars and creating its own.

Dorian J. Sinnott's work has appeared in over 250 journals and has been nominated for the Best of the Net.

For Telematic Eyes Only by Jameson Grey

Gibson did not panic.

Although the left eye had gone into shutdown, the backup lens would soon restore full vision. But was there enough time?

Tasks (broadly): espionage, sabotage.

Known unknown: probability of being a one-way mission.

The satellite sweep had been successful, airdropping Gibson in right on the mark, allowing precious minutes to transmit the vital information to central processing. Before long, though, the enemy would arrive.

Gibson was prepared.

An alarm nearby sounded. Voices followed. Too late for escape now, Gibson thought, readying the self-destruct sequence with which all cyborgs were primed.

The humans were coming for him.

* * *

Originally published in *Ctrl Alt Del* (Black Ink Fiction) in April of 2022.

* * *

Jameson Grey's work has been published in numerous anthologies. He can be found online at jameson-grey.com and on Twitter @thejamesongrey

Constellation by Leigh Loveday

I stand in the street and feel it hungry and heavy on my neck. A vile sigil scratched into the night. A defamation of heaven.

The shotgun wards off those who've looked up. Some do it intentionally now. My father did, ever the scientist. Then he tried to kill his whole family and almost succeeded.

I still hear ragged screams across town. Sirens, too, but not as many. Civilisation wanes every night.

I'll stay here as long as I can. Eventually I'll use the shotgun. Or just raise my eyes.

Maybe, at the end, I'll understand why we deserved this.

Leigh Loveday edits videogame marketing blurb by day, and writes fiction aggressively slowly by night. Find him on Twitter @MrLovelyday.

Parallel Landings by Kai Holmwood

At first, Delmar had feared being alone. Ten years on a space mission is a long time.

Later, as a silver shape approached his ship impossibly quickly, he faced the opposite fear.

Both fears proved unnecessary. Solitude became comfortable; meetings with intergalactic life were always peaceful.

It never occurred to him to fear returning.

When he landed, no one came to meet him. His childhood home was gone. His wife didn't recognize his face, or even their daughter's name.

Of infinite alternate worlds, Delmar had accidentally reached one in which he had never existed—and his rudder was irreparably broken.

Kai Holmwood, an MA in Writing graduate from the University of Canterbury, splits her time between New Zealand and Portugal.

Underneath the Broken Mountain by Dana Vickerson

I told Reese we had no business going in. Three moons rose beyond the cracked outline of the mountain, looking like a warning.

He always played games. Practical jokes. Guess being stuck on a desolate rock with my ugly mug had him stir crazy. We'd been down there twenty minutes when he went silent. Thought he was hiding or some shit.

I did find him in the end. Those pink fucking tendrils coming out of the rock. Never seen anything like that. How they ate away his suit, his skin, his eyes.

I told him we never shoulda gone in.

Dana's work appears in many Shacklebound anthologies and other places. You can find her on Twitter @dmvickerson.

Salesman of the Month by Rohan Magerman

"What kind of sick joke is this?"

Ignoring Jeremy's hostility, the salesman pressed on with his pitch: "We can recreate your wife as a lifelike hologram that you can talk to and interact with as if she were still alive."

Jeremy's eyes burned with rage. "Leave!"

The door slammed shut. The salesman wedged his business card into the doorframe.

He'll come around, he assured himself. *They always do.*

He loosened his tie, winching slightly as the fabric grazed the gashes where she'd clawed at his throat.

Now, only three more lives to end before he'd make this month's sales quota.

Rohan is a passionate sci-fi enthusiast and storyteller, seeking to make a dent in the universe with his words.

The Rhytholean Cryptex by Coby Rosser

The last artifact pulled from the ruins of planet Rhythos was a marvelously crafted apparatus much like DaVinci's cylindrical puzzle container. Professor of Alien Archeology and Rhytholean civilization expert, Dr. Caballero, studied the piece meticulously, making hypotheses about what might be locked inside, and why it'd been held in a secure vault several miles beneath the planet's surface.

Working with fine-tuned, controllable appendages from behind a safety barrier, he manipulated the artifact, rotating its alien rune engraved combinations to computer suggested patterns. Upon solving the cryptex, however, the planet Rhythos and everything within its solar system vanished without a trace.

Coby Rosser is a weathered IT guy from the southern US. He writes speculatively and plays guitar. Tweet him @paperninjaman

Food Processor Blues by Coby Rosser

It'd been 27 days since the collision, but an estimated 6 years, 2 months, and 3 weeks remained on the return voyage. Roshelle—once again—took to studying the ship's food processing unit's manuals. Biomolecular chemistry and quantum printing mechanics weren't her strong suit, but as the ship's only surviving atomics engineer, the remaining crew looked to her in desperation.

Beside her, the disgusting brown gruel they'd been forced to eat since the accident crawled about in a bowl. All necessary nutrients were present, but it severely lacked in flavor and un-life. Some had even started calling the substance mana.

Coby Rosser is a weathered IT guy from the southern US. He writes speculatively and plays guitar. Tweet him @paperninjaman

Vessel Breached; Requesting Aid by Addison Smith

Aboard the ship the hull doesn't creak. Its metal is torn, ripped apart by strange claws that melt through metal, give way to bodies that resist our bullets and knives. Acid burns my helmet and I cry silent into my comm. The door opens, a hand gripping it with human dexterity. I can only pray my message went through. As the creature steps into the room, my prayers die in my heart.

It lifts a comm to a face like my own. "Cancel request," it says. "Just seeing things."

The creature turns to face me, skull splitting into a grin.

Addison Smith knows that in space they can't hear him scream, but still he cries into the void. He tweets @AddisonCSmith

Different, Distant Stars by Patricia Miller

The sun is not quite the same shade of yellow as Sol, just a hint larger. Most people would be unable to tell the difference. Many would swear there *was* no difference. The skies were still blue, the grass still green.

I stand on the coast of an ancient azure sea, many light years from Terra, gazing at constellations distorted by space and perspective, no longer recognizable. The exhaust of the ship has faded from the deep black sky.

Stranded, I have no chance of returning to see the stars of home again. The growls behind me grow ever closer.

Patricia writes science fiction, fantasy, and horror and is currently in the query trenches with a middle grade ghost story.

Don't Mind Me, I'm Just a Rock by Wondra Vanian

The problem with the human race's ignorance was that arrogance often accompanied it. The problem with the human race's expansion into space was that they took that ignorance with them.

Humans believed two things. One, that they would recognize an alien lifeform if they came across one and two, that they would be both strong enough and smart enough to overcome it.

The first alien they came across proved them wrong on both counts.

The crew that came behind to clean up the mess were... only human.

"Hey, look," one called as he picked up the amused alien. "Cool rock!"

Wondra Vanian is an American who lives in the UK with her partner and their mischief of sausage dogs.

The Shortest Distance Between Two Points
by Giancarlo Makashi

Chris looked at his wrist. Oxygen, 92.3%.

The cobalt pulse pushed him away from the ship, but didn't hurt him. It probably killed Zazie, but he'd never know.

No, from here on, it was just Newton's First Law for him. They'd been working on the outer edge, in the blind. No one was coming.

He started his timer a minute or two after he'd regained his senses. That was 1:36:22 ago, when Oxygen was 92.4%. New tech. Oxygen lasted forever now.

Not forever. Just 66.92 more days.

I wonder how far I'll go, he thought.

Giancarlo is a writer with a black belt in Northern Eagle Claw Kung Fu and the poetry of T.S. Eliot.

Take Me by Ryan Brinson

I smile as it takes me.

I begged for this and as I feel it coil around me, I exhale in relief. Oily and tight against the hairs on my chest, it's coating and recreating my body with its slick blackness. A euphoric burst in my fingertips. I finally feel strong.

Then, a sting. My vision blurs and muscles go slack. Panic begs me to protest but it's too late. It's refashioning my mind as its own. I gasp, taking in the darkness of its hot breath, and in the final eyeblink of who I was, I scream my regret.

Ryan Brinson lives in New York, likes dinosaurs, nachos, bookstores, and The Haunted Mansion, and can always be found writing.

Also by Shacklebound Books

Short Horror Stories
Short Horror Stories is an anthology of horror drabbles, stories of exactly 100 words. Within its pages are dark morsels, creepy moments, and spooky, spine chilling tales.

Planetside: Science Fiction Drabbles
Planetside is an anthology of drabbles, stories of exactly 100 words. Within these pages are micro science fiction stories from Liam Hogan, Marc Criley, Michelle Ann King, Marisca Pichette, Anna Madden, and many, many others!

Chronos: An Anthology of Time Drabbles
Chronos is an anthology of drabbles (a story told in exactly one-hundred words) themed around time. Seventy-five talented authors from around the world come together to present ninety-eight stories of time, time travel, time zones, time manipulation, flash-forwards, space-time, time freezes, and so many other variations on the theme.

Drabbledark II: An Anthology of Dark Drabbles

Drabbledark II is an anthology of dark science fiction, dark fantasy, and dark horror drabbles, stories of exactly 100 words. Within its pages are dark morsels of other worlds by Michelle Ann King, Liam Hogan, Ai Jiang, Dorian J. Sinnott, Joachim Heijndermans, Jacob Steven Mohr, and many others!